COUNTRY MUSIC
Night Before Christmas

# COUNTRY MUSIC
## Night Before Christmas

**Written by Thomas N. Turner**

**Illustrated by James Rice**

**PELICAN PUBLISHING COMPANY**
Gretna 2003

*To Nancy Turner, my wife and pure inspiration, and James E. Akenson,*
*who knows more about country-music history than*
*anyone and was willing to share that knowledge*

*The word "Pelican" and the depiction of a pelican are trademarks*
*of Pelican Publishing Company, Inc., and are registered*
*in the U.S. Patent and Trademark Office.*

**Library of Congress Cataloging-in-Publication Data**

Turner, Thomas Noel.
  Country music Night before Christmas / written by Thomas N. Turner ;
illustrated by James Rice.
       p. cm.
Summary: An adaptation in mountain dialect of the well-known poem about
an important Christmas visitor.
  ISBN 1-58980-148-2
  1. Children's poetry, American. 2. Christmas--Juvenile poetry. 3.
Santa Claus--Juvenile poetry. 4. Country life--Juvenile poetry. [1.
Santa Claus--Poetry. 2. Christmas--Poetry. 3. Narrative poetry. 4.
American poetry.] I. Rice, James, ill. II. Title.
  PS3570.U735C68 2003
  811'.54—dc21

                                    2003009210

Printed in China
Published by Pelican Publishing Company, Inc.
1000 Burmaster Street, Gretna, Louisiana 70053

## COUNTRY MUSIC NIGHT BEFORE CHRISTMAS

Christmas Eve came a humming around Nashville town,
Where carols are played with that great country sound
From fiddles and banjos and guitars and drums,
Where "Rudolph" and "Frosty" are plucked, picked, and strummed.

Up and down Music Row, it had started in snowing;
No one cared 'cause the Oprey was just getting going.
All along Printers' Alley, the neon shone bright,
And everywhere, Christmas was all bustle and light.

Our house was a natural wonder to see,
With big plastic wreaths and aluminum trees;
In all the front windows we'd painted snowflakes.
We'd hung plastic stockings and put out fruitcakes.

The kids—really pumped—had been hugged into bed.
Dreams of cool Christmas presents danced in each head—
Of videos, keyboards, and electric guitars—
Why, they'd soon get discovered and become Nashville stars.

My wife in her housecoat and me in my sweats,
Both flopped on the couch by two big TV sets.
She held the popcorn and I the remotes;
Life couldn't get better if I got me two boats.

With a great blast of feedback we all were just rocked—
A buzz, then a screech, then a pop, snap that shocked.
We scrambled and screamed; our stuff flew everywhere.
We'll be sweeping up popcorn well into next year.

We both crawled to the window and ripped down the curtain
To stare out, not knowing what we'd see for certain.
The moon was just peeping o'er Tennessee hills.
Our jaws dropped in surprise; what we saw gave us chills.

Our neighbors had strung about three jillion lights,
Plus angels and snowmen and other fine sights;
Their electronic extravagance made it seem like day.
(Come New Year's we'd all have big light bills to pay.)

All those lights lit the world like our own private star,
And high in the sky was a red muscle car.
It came through the snow with a drumroll and roar—
A '56 Caddy with four on the floor.

With a driver in Raybans who gave it the gun—
If he'd been at Daytona, that old boy might have won.
And we knew in a flash as he drove, hammer down,
That this was old Santa, not some rodeo clown.

Standing out on the hood, wearing huge cowboy hats,
Was a big backup band of great Nashville cats.
Their "surround-car" sound system had amplification
To make Nashville their stage—and maybe the nation.

An elf ran the soundboard from the Caddy's back fin,
And his genius for mixing was pure country sin.
Santa laughed at the wheel with a South-North Pole drawl,
And with a blare of the horn, he called, "Hello, y'all!"

Hank

Marty

Tammy

Ernest

Bill

Jimmy

Grampa

He named all his band, which inspired me with joy.
"There's 'Hello, darlin',' Conway and 'Orange Blossom' Roy;
And Patsy and Hank could sure sing about cheatin',
And Marty with stories of gunfighters meetin'."

"Old Ernest was walkin' the floor over you,
While Tammy stood by her man and was true.
And Bob was the best with that great Texas swing,
And Floyd could sure make those piano keys ring.

"If you had some money, then Lefty had time;
Jimmy could yodel, and Grampa could rhyme.
Bill's the best that there was with a fine bluegrass tune;
Tex sang about heaven and also high noon."

Cross the whole Nashville skyline they came in a flash.
With a skid, Santa slid 'til we thought he would crash!
Then he sang to the band, "Now, don't play the bridge slow.
We'll give them one set, and then we've got to go!"

With a screeching of brakes, as the band tapped their toes,
They were up on our roof and went on with their show.
I looked at my wife, and she asked me, "What's next?
Rock-a-billy, line dancin', or maybe Tex-Mex?"

Then a new voice resounded, saying, "Let's hear it now!
Let the North Pole's own legend come on for a bow!
Put your two hands together. . . ." (He got loud and then paused.)
"Give a big Nashville welcome to the best—Santa Claus!"

And then while we stood there, way too stunned to react,
Down the chimney came Santa—it's pure country fact.
I don't know how he does it all over the globe,
But he makes a grand entrance with spotlights and strobes.

He was decked out pure Western from his boots to his hat,
But no cowhand I've seen ever wore duds like that.
From the top of his head to the tip of his toes,
He looked like old Porter had picked out his clothes.

His boots were red leather, all studded in gold.
White jeans and white shirt—what a sight to behold!
Cross the back of his coat was a sequined guitar;
On his red cowboy hat was a big rhinestone star.

And then in a moment, the band filled the room
With a sound that was bigger than ten sonic booms.
I don't know what they played or even what key,
But I tell you, I sure wish I had that CD!

Then Santa himself made our house center stage,
With a grin that would fill any book, page by page.
Setting down his big pack, he pulled out a string bass
And played all the brightly wrapped presents in place.

With each pluckity plunk, the packages flew,
For the children and me and their sweet mama too.
Each gift moved, on the beat, to a place 'neath the tree
Or the right Christmas stocking—it was something to see!

And when he was done, Santa went to the tag,
Put his big bass away, and then picked up his bag.
While we clapped, Santa exited—chimney, stage right.
Santa had left the building, gone into the night.

He revved up that big Caddy and eased it in gear,
And he shouted for everyone list'ning to hear.
"Happy Christmas, y'all! See you same time, same place!
Keep the love in your heart and a smile on your face!"

"I thought that the world and all Nashville should know
Where old country-music stars go when they go.
It seemed such a natural thing up in heaven
For folks with such love to keep givin' and givin'."

I rushed out the door—just to give him a yell,
Hollered, "Don't be a stranger! Come on back! Set a spell!"
And I heard his last shout, just before he got gone.
"We'll all have a big time! You just leave the light on!"